PURGATORY

-MIKE SCHUHLER-

First Printing, 2022
ISBN 978-1-937272-11-1

COVER BY
Francois Vaillancourt
EDITING BY
Lyndsey Smith with Horrorsmith Editing
www.Horrorsmithediting.com
INTERIOR FORMATTING AND DESIGN BY
Melissa Stevens with The Illustrated Author Design
www.theillustratedauthor.com

Dark Jester Publishing
3760 Piazza Dr, #107
Fort Myers, FL 33916
www.TheDarkJester.com

CHAPTER
- ONE -

Grant Radburn was waiting in his living room when Trevor arrived in the late afternoon. The house smelled familiar—spicy notes of roasted chicken combined with the scent of a fireplace—and it was in good order, at least better than it had been the last time Trevor visited.

Trevor Martin had driven the two hours from Ann Arbor, at Grant's last-minute request, to discuss something of urgent matter. He had known Grant for some time. It wasn't lost on anyone that Grant was a lonely man, a widower, something they shared in common, aside from their love of both whiskey and hockey.

"'Bout damn time you got here," Grant said. He was sitting in his old leather chair, half-facing the fireplace. Across from it was the matching loveseat draped in a knitted yellow blanket.

"My apologies, you old goat. Highway construction again." Trevor sat down on the loveseat. "But I made it."

Grant stood. "Drink?"

"Does a bear sh—"

"Oh, shut the hell up. One second." Grant walked to the small bar on the wall opposite the fireplace. "Cigar?"

"Of course." Trevor pulled his jacket off and set it beside him. "So...what's the big deal? Why am I here?"

Grant refrained from speaking as he poured a short glass of Jameson.

"Well...," he said, handing the glass to Trevor. "Men gotta talk sometimes." He slid over a cigar box with a trembling hand.

"Talk? Grant, you never been one for talking." Trevor opened the box and retrieved a single cigar, cut the tip, and lit it. Ribbons of smoke curled to the ceiling. "What's going on?"

Grant sipped from his glass. "Devon. It's about Devon."

"Devon? Haven't heard from him in years," Trevor said, rolling the cigar between his thumb and index finger. "What's going on with him?"

"What I am about to tell you...it stays here." Strands of long silver hair hung over Grant's face as he looked to the floor.

"Sure...of course."

Grant's chest expanded with a deep breath. "He's dead."

"Jesus, what happened?" Trevor asked, placing the cigar in an ashtray.

"I...I killed him." With an old, quivering hand, Grant brought the half-full glass of warm whiskey to his lips and swallowed the remaining contents.

"You did? You killed that asshole? Why? How?" Trevor's face hung in disbelief.

"A manner of speaking, yes," Grant said. "And his boy too."

"Paul?"

Grant nodded. The fireplace cracked, sending glowing embers dancing into the air before they disappeared.

"Grant, why are you telling me this?" Trevor stood and walked to the bar, grabbing the green bottle of Irish whiskey. "I mean, wasn't Devon a friend of yours? Why would you...you know—"

"Kill them? The *place* took them. All I did was bring them there," Grant explained, sliding his glass across the coffee table to be filled.

"The place? Buddy, you need to start making sense." Trevor sat down once more. His bald head wore a dull shine in the dim light of the fire. "What place? You didn't take him to that Coney Island in the city, did you?" he added with a chuckle. "That'll kill anyone."

The humor failed to make a landing.

Grant ran a hand through his hair and thought deeply. "They came to me. I knew the bastard was a murderer, and I helped him for so many years, and—"

"Whoa, whoa...Slow down, man," Trevor said, patting Grant's forearm with an outstretched palm. "Obviously, we have a lot to unpack here. Relax and start from the beginning."

Hidden within the darkness of the dining room, a chime sounded. The haunting toll of the grandfather clock indicated the passage of another hour.

With the strike of a match, Grant's face glowed within a gently dancing halo as he brought the flame to a fresh cigar. "He came to me with the body of dead girl..."

CHAPTER
- TWO -

Nightmares. They seldom last more than a few moments, and like a flame caught in a chilling gust, they fade and ultimately die. If we are lucky, they are forgotten. But sometimes, those refuse to die, and this particular one has haunted me for decades, will remain long after I am gone.

In the early morning, we had set off from the foggy shores of Michigan's Upper Peninsula. It was still dark then—cold and dark. It would be another two hours before the sun even began to spray the sky with the pinkish hue of dawn. Silhouettes of distant ships dotted the horizon, greeting the world with their mellow horns.

We had grown old, Devon and I. Seeing him after so long had surprised me a bit, not because our friendship had dwindled over the years, but because he just looked…old. His former mane of greasy, jet-black hair had been replaced by a neatly trimmed salt and pepper crew cut. His face, a bit more grizzled but just like my own, had been hidden beneath a thick beard. He was always the more dapper type between the two of us.

Devon MacArthur had been a longtime friend of mine since high school, though life had taken us down different paths—his destiny much more neatly wrapped than mine. My entry into adulthood was laden with the hot and humid darkness of a jungle I never knew existed, an experience amounting to fuck-all in the end.

Devon went off to college in Chicago, where he shook the right hands that led him to become one wealthy son of a bitch by the age of thirty. I would be lying if I said I didn't hold some kind of resentment toward him over that, even after all these years.

His son, Paul, was a different story. Honestly, I would have preferred for him be the one wrapped up in a tarp below deck. Instead, Paul was lying on the tattered old seat inside the cabin, napping away waves of nausea.

I wish things had gone differently between us, but our longtime friendship had faded many years ago, well before it took on a more *professional* relationship. It wasn't until much later I realized this man had been poisonous.

It was on that day—that cold October day—I had decided to gain some closure.

"Grant, I owe you big time for this," Devon said as he leaned over to get a better view. His hand patted my shoulder and disappeared. "I mean it."

Those words coming from Devon's mouth had been repeated countless times since departing the familiar old dock located just outside of Copper Harbor. I'd grown tired of his constant expression of gratitude and ceased acknowledging it some time ago, hoping for peace and quiet.

My tired eyes remained focused on the water ahead. Lake Superior was choppy and cold, especially this time of year, when the leaves back home turned color and the air had a clean, crisp feel to it.

The engine fumes reawakened the old sailor in me, while nauseating the other two. They weren't built for life on the water, even for half a day. Out on the lake, frigid gusts delivered a frosty bite, allowing me to ignore Devon's occasional reminder of the favor. A favor for him and his waste of a son, who had developed sea sickness quite early, much to my enjoyment.

The trawler was questionably outdated, a loaner from another old friend of mine who used to help me out prior to retiring. The light-colored deck had been stained with dirt and grime over the years. The cabin lacked the bells and whistles of modern boats but had all I needed to get us to that awful place—heat and cold beer.

The navigation equipment and weather station were nice but effectively useless. Lake Superior was known for its temper changes, luring you in with a nice day, only to send you headfirst into a massive storm that might doom you to a watery grave.

It didn't take long before the Upper Peninsula shoreline had disappeared and land was nowhere in sight. Hours would pass before we would see any of the familiar islands dotting a very specific route. Devon and Paul spent much of the time asleep, leaving me to my thoughts as I listened to an old Bob Seger tape I had thankfully remembered to grab before leaving.

I piloted across the expanse of the massive lake, realizing how long it had been since I last came out this way. *Shortly after she passed*, I thought.

After Lori died, I stopped going out on the water. Sold the boat and everything. I would trade all those days spent away, fishing, for just another hour with her.

Fishing conjured a strange kind of solitude I couldn't handle after the reaper made me a widower. I suppose solitude lost its meaning once I was forced to live it all the time. Those days somehow only got harder, like the ones you wake up and read the paper, only to find the obituary littered with familiar names, like Tom Hayes and Lennie Stevens from the lodge. Or Valerie Fishman, who died last year from a stroke. I remember dating her in high school, before the draft notice came and saw an end to that.

I sat white-knuckled, with tired, arthritic hands steering the trawler through choppy waters rocking and swaying us. That was when Devon and Paul started their groaning, as the threat of motion sickness resurfaced. The lake had a way of disposing the unlucky and foolish who dared to brave it at its worst, like the poor souls of the *Fitzgerald*. But it wasn't just the lake that made me nervous.

The charcoal black waters blanketing this region of Superior hid many secrets, our destination being one of them. Perhaps its darkest. Rumors plagued the area, such as underground caverns beneath the lake itself. The island I had set our heading for was one of trepidation and buried secrets—the kind that carry a price. It was located in an area tucked away, possibly by God himself, as if it were some kind of abomination.

As we continued on our way to that awful place, outside lay the reason I found myself making the trip once more. A trip I once said I would never take again, but deep down, I knew I would have to again one day.

No one knew her name—the body of the young woman who died at Paul's hands not even a day prior. They both insisted it was an accident, but I knew better. This wasn't his first accident, not the first time I had to clean up his mess. One thing I do know for sure is, somewhere out there is a family missing their daughter, or someone missing a wife or girlfriend…even worse, a mother.

I couldn't think of these things, as it made what was to come much worse. What a dark deed this truly was.

Things began to change when closing in on the island.

From a distance, the eye couldn't tell it even existed.

The air became thick and hazy, with a wall of unearthly fog hanging above the water—the first sign that we were near. It curled around the hull and infiltrated my senses with that unmistakable wretched stink, carrying a slight peppery tinge that left the eyes watery and the throat parched for fresh water. The fog was only the first of many features making up such an unnatural and vile place. Thankfully, the cabin prevented much of the wretched mist from making me completely miserable.

"Found some fog, or what?" Devon asked, fighting back a cough.

"It'll clear. Try not to breathe too much of it, though," I cautioned.

"Hope so. Smells terrible."

Just you wait, old friend, I thought.

The mist formed swirling tendrils around the trawler before being absorbed back into oblivion as we ventured deeper through the smoky wall. I used a knit cap that reeked of tobacco to cover my face so I could breathe easier, while Paul joined Devon in fighting back coughing fits.

"Like breathing in ginger ale, eh?" Devon jested before breaking out into a cough once more. "How can you see through all that?" His voice got scratchy and irritated.

"Can't see shit. And we won't until we get through," I said, trying to focus through watery eyes.

Back in the cabin, Paul's coughing grew more intense. "Jesus, what is—" He stopped to clear his throat. "What is this shit? Tear gas?"

I imagined his boyish face contorted in pain, with tears streaming down his pale, hairless cheeks as he wretched. "Might as well be," I said.

Devon sat in the seat beside me. "So…what do these buttons do?" He chuckled as he fingered over the various gauges and buttons in front of him. The lights in the wheelhouse dimmed and brightened. "Oops, guess that answers that one."

I fought back a grin. "You're a pain in my ass."

His face creased and wrinkled with a genuine laugh. "Like a bad case of hemorrhoids."

I chuckled. "Hemorrhoids go away, at least."

The engine carried us slowly through the sickening mist, and our destination was revealed in the distance. The water was inky black, and the wind carried with it a unique chill, making living flesh feel almost dead to the touch. Exposed skin took on a cold, lifeless appearance similar to wet clay. This place, whatever it really was, was not supposed to be here. I knew that much.

"Is that it?" Devon asked.

The response I wanted to give him was "no," but the one that came from my mouth, "Sure is."

Part of me wanted to turn around right there and abandon the whole idea. Perhaps just dump her overboard and call it a day. As grisly and heartless as it sounded, it was still a better option than what the original plan called for.

Devon wouldn't go for it anyhow. He would know better—he always did. Devon was a scoundrel, a snake. That's how he did business. Steven Dewey, an old associate of his, learned the hard way after being thrown from the top of a luxury apartment tower. Chalked up as a suicide, and then Devon profited. Not to mention the other "disposals" Devon paid me to do for him over the years. The ones no one knew of.

My stomach sank as we neared the dreadful place. My old bones trembled under the weight of terror I carried with me that very moment. There was no mistaking the mountain sitting high above the water on one end, overlooking the rest of the heavily wooded area with eerie stillness. Overall, the island was enormous. Its shape created treacherous currents that could easily drag a person to the depths below, never to be seen again.

Paul's coughing had gotten worse. He heaved and gagged.

"Sounds like you should go check on him. Water should help," I said.

Devon looked over his shoulder. "Paul…you gonna survive, or what?" With no response other than a coughing fit, he stood. "Be right back."

Our ears popped from the sudden change in pressure as we approached. It was a painful experience, typical of visiting the place, but a short-lived one that went away after crossing a certain point in the water. I always imagined some kind of invisible barrier or threshold surrounding the island.

My breathing grew shallow with heightened anxiety, knowing I somehow found this place with little aid, as if it guided me here itself. I couldn't forget this island no matter how old I got. Perhaps even with a strong case of dementia, I would somehow find myself standing on its cursed shores.

Ahead of us, closer to the island, the water was rough. Whitecaps littered the choppy surface. I took a deep breath and prepared myself for what would be nothing short of a battle.

With the music gone, I listened to the engine as it drew us closer. Low, subtle grumbling from the clouds overhead stirred up more restlessness within me. A storm would make this trip harder than it already was.

I steered us closer, a smoke gripped between my lips. The bow of the trawler bobbed up and down aggressively over increasingly large waves that threatened to pour over onto the deck. My gut had been rocked by the chaos, but I fought through it. The two behind me grew ill from the violent motion of the water.

"I'm gonna get sick if this—" Nausea swam over him like a hot blanket, and Devon was silenced.

"Just hold on," I said. My palms sweat under the grip of the wheel. My back tightened, and my throat dried with fiery nerves.

The bow rose high and immediately dropped, jostling my head around like a toy doll. The waters surrounding the island were littered with rocky protrusions, posing a hazard to anyone not seasoned enough to navigate them. Waves continued to drag the trawler as the engine fought against them, narrowly missing one of the large rocks towering above the angry water.

Whitecaps surrounded the large boat and swelled into angry crests. The windshield had come under constant assault from wind and water spray, and the wipers couldn't keep up.

"Christ, Grant, are we gonna make it?" Devon asked, gripping the seat hard to not be tossed from it.

The wheel fought me as I steered. "Come on. Almost there," I said, clenching my jaw as the bow dipped into a steep trough. Waves crashed onto the deck, sending a cascade of water over the windshield. I corrected the trawler and pushed the engine a little harder.

We entered the seclusion of the small cove where I could safely anchor, and the waves suddenly calmed. The dim lighting of the wheelhouse took on a stronger yellow hue as the sky overhead darkened. I took a deep breath, realizing we were about to leave the only true refuge we had.

If the other two knew the things I did, they wouldn't dare leave the boat.

CHAPTER
- THREE -

I cut off the engine and stepped outside to set anchor as close to the shore as I could bring us.

Leaving the cabin had exposed us to the truly dreadful environment. The shoreline, pungent with the aroma of wet earth, had been entirely covered by dull black sand. Broken trees and rotted timber poked through the surface, as if the sand had been slowly digesting it over the years.

"Never seen a beach like that before," Paul said, his thin arms clutching tightly around his body. "Freezing out here."

"Shit, it stinks too," Devon added, his face scrunched in disgust. "Please tell me it gets better."

The air was musty, filling our nostrils with a powerful, acrid stench.

"You'll get used to it." I lit a smoke and took in the sight. The bitter wind cut like razors into my bare hands.

"So, how do we get over there? Have a raft or something?" Paul asked in that terrible, nasally voice of his. "I can't swim...that good, at least."

"You should be able to touch the bottom. Don't worry." I gathered the rest of my pack and prepared to leave the boat.

One by one, we each left the safety of the trawler and dropped into the frigid water, leaving Devon last to handle the corpse.

"This water is...Holy shit. I can barely breathe," Paul said.

"Come on and grab onto that end," Devon instructed Paul as he dragged the girl's body over the rail and into the icy water.

He was frustrated, but I ignored the tension between the two and focused on moving through what felt like a gauntlet of icy razor blades hidden beneath the tide.

The strong current we fought against forced us to move slowly at an angle. The sand made it a challenge to reach the shoreline. It had little resistance and would cave underfoot. One wrong move would send me below the water, to be dragged away by the current.

This was the last place I would want to die.

After what felt like an eternity, I reached the shore and watched them move in from the waist-high water, carrying the girl's body still wrapped in the old tarp. They were slow and miserable. This place had a special ability to break a man's spirit quickly. I stood there with the woods to my back and fished through my small backpack for the one thing that could bring me some clarity. Within moments, I had a freshly lit cigarette hanging from my dry, wind-chapped lips. Smoke curled in ribbons in front of my eyes as I watched the two struggle ashore, making no effort to help drag that corpse onto the beach.

That was their burden—Paul's burden.

They stood near me, curiously taking in the environment, and stared into the thick woods blanketing the island. It was heavily overgrown with towering pines and old white ash.

"This place smells rotten," Devon said, cupping a hand over his nose and mouth.

A light wind tossed the short locks of black and white hair around his face. Paul had his back to us, watching the water beyond the cove. Its appearance was even more treacherous from here as waves rose up and crashed around rocks.

"Where to from here?" Devon asked, looking around for some sort of path or roadway.

With an outstretched arm, fingers gripping my smoke, I pointed at the large rock formation peeking over the tree-tops. "That mountain over there."

Both of their spirits collapsed in front of me upon realizing the task at hand. Devon took in a deep breath as he eyed the rocky peak jutting over the wooded expanse. Paul dropped his shoulders, and disappointment washed over his face.

"That is not close at all," Devon said.

"How are we supposed to get out there?" Paul's small frame slumped with disbelief.

"You follow me out there. This is not going to be easy. But it is the only way to get there from here," I said.

"Is there at least a trail or something?" Devon asked.

"Nope. That's why it'll be important to take our time and watch where we step." I tossed the cigarette butt to the ground. "You'll both need to take turns carrying her out there."

"Shouldn't be too bad. She weighs at most a hundred or so," Paul said.

Devon looked at Paul in a way that could only convey disappointment. I could tell he knew something about Paul that he really didn't like. Paul had shown no remorse for this girl, talked about her as if he had been checking baggage at an airport.

"Yeah, shouldn't be too bad. Maybe you should take her first, eh?" Devon suggested.

As the two decided who would carry the girl first, I took the moment to soak in where I stood once again. With the water to my back, I found myself feeling hopeless and even a bit afraid. The trees and the brush…the rocks…it was all an illusion—a mockery of nature. The place was an abomination. The edge of the woods was thick with brush. Brown vines coiled around trees and laced through the undergrowth, resembling alien-like tendrils that had been armed with excessively long, black thorns, making the forest nearly impenetrable.

"Watch out for the thorns. They hurt like a son of a bitch," I warned.

Devon followed close behind. "Those look mean as hell."

"They have a scratch that'll irritate you for hours too."

"Noted," Devon said.

Behind us trailed Paul, who struggled getting the corpse through the thick vegetation. "Can I get some help here?" he called out to his father.

Already needing someone else to help him. He was useless, completely and utterly useless.

Devon turned back and helped drag the corpse through so Paul could get better situated.

"The brush thins out a bit once you're through," I said, waiting for them to catch up.

The smell of wet earth had mingled with the rotten pine needles clustered on the soft woodland floor, a stench increasing in potency the deeper we ventured.

Our movement was quickly hindered by the treacherous landscape. Paul and Devon took short turns carrying the girl. I knew all too well the pains experienced from having to shoulder the weight of a soggy, wet corpse. Grunts and a myriad of cursing followed behind me as we navigated the first uphill climb through twisted, stinging vegetation.

"I can't see shit out here," Paul said, slowing his stride.

I looked back to see their shadowy figures trailing farther apart than they had been. "The canopy is too thick, blocks out most of the light. You need to stay close, or you'll get lost for sure."

My wet clothes had weighed me down for some time, and to say I was uncomfortable would be an understatement. My boots had been rubbing me raw, and my shirt clung to me like moist plastic wrap. Somehow, I had forgotten how miserable this experience was, regardless of preparation or equipment. I sucked it up and sipped water as the two behind me suffered their own personal journey.

"Sounds like the storm is getting closer," Devon said.

He wasn't wrong. Storms frequented the region, and it wouldn't be long before we had one right on top of us.

"Ah, yeah. I wouldn't be surprised if it started pissin' down soon," I said.

"Oh, great." Paul grunted under the corpse's weight.

"Rain'll make this ground like walking on a damn sponge. We'll be miserable for sure then," I said, adjusting the straps of my pack.

Devon's voice was closer now and heavy with sarcasm. "Thanks for the heads-up. I'm looking forward to it."

"This place is confusing as hell. How do we find our way through here?" Devon adjusted the weight of the corpse on his shoulders after taking it from Paul. "And all of these ravines. This is killing me. I nearly broke my ankle back there on some exposed tree roots," he added.

"I told you this wasn't gonna be easy. I wasn't kidding," I said. My eyes burned with fatigue, reminding me to take a strong gulp of water that had taken on the dull taste of plastic.

The way ahead promised nothing different. The twisted limbs and exposed roots of trees whose ages numbered in the hundreds had been a common hazard here.

"Just trust me." I wish I had a better answer, and maybe I did. Honestly, I really didn't want to get into how many times I'd been through here, or how it was always a little different each time.

"Feels like we've gone in every direction so far," Paul said over the sound of twigs and brush snapping underfoot.

The canopy spiderwebbed overhead. The little bit of sunlight that hadn't been choked out blended with the lingering misty haze of twilight, blanketing us in a valley of slow-churning smoky shadows familiar only to a nightmarish palette bearing the colors of impending dusk.

"Orienting toward the mountain is near impossible. Too many areas are impassable, and we'd be hunting for ways around all day and into the night. Only one good way to get there," I said.

"How far away is this place we're going?" Devon's face had grown blotchy and red.

"Few miles," I replied. "It'll feel like a dozen by the time we get there."

We pressed on, and pain crept through my joints. The air chilled flesh, like we were stuck in a morgue, yet sweat ran down my back and collected on my forehead as if I were humping through a stagnant, humid jungle. I couldn't think of carrying a corpse through this...not at my age, at least.

If it were up to me, Paul would carry her the entire way. Fortunately, it was not my cross to bear.

I checked my watch but remembered how time meant nothing here. The minutes moved at a crawl, practically stopping entirely. The hands had barely moved since we crossed the threshold of the fog.

"Hey, I have to rest," Devon said, carefully easing the corpse to the ground from his shoulder.

It was intimate, the way he carried the girl. I recognized his agony, the way his face contorted with the pain of dead weight bearing down on his frame. The man was clearly exhausted, his clothes darkened from sweat.

Paul rested himself against the trunk of an old birch. If I were his father, I couldn't help but feel utter disappointment in such a weak display.

I fished a smoke from my pocket and lit it before getting my bearings.

"How much farther?" Devon asked.

"Not sure." I struggled with the answer, unable to remember how long it'd taken before. "Maybe an hour or so."

"Looks like were losing daylight," Devon said.

The smoke stung my throat and clouded my senses. "We'll be fine."

Gusts of wind kicked through the tree branches above us, bringing our attention to the canopy.

"You know what? I haven't seen any birds or anything here yet," Paul said.

"You won't." I tossed my cigarette to the ground. "Nothing lives here. Nothing at all."

Devon immediately wore a cautious grin, as if I were exaggerating. "Come on. That can't be true."

I felt my hair stand up on end with a slight tinge of anger. "Take a look around, old friend. Listen. You hear anything?"

"No, man. Take it easy, will you," Devon replied.

I turned to Paul. "Hear anything?"

His face hung in a stupor. "Uh, no. I don't hear shit."

I nodded in agreement, adjusting my pack. "This place is dead. Best you realize that now."

CHAPTER
- FOUR -

Within the passage of another hour, we found ourselves deeper in the woods but felt as if no progress had been made. The ancient and narrow paths would appear and fade into oblivion, forcing me to lead them through thick vegetation in hopes of finding some kind of trail once cleared. I tried to avoid the snare of hidden shrubs and exposed roots with each step through the ever-darkening labyrinth. At this point, I couldn't tell where the hell we were, but I had to trust we were making progress.

"I can't do this anymore." Devon stopped, entangled in sticks and overgrowth. "Paul, take her. I can't carry her any further."

Paul, appearing frustrated and tired, turned and walked back to retrieve the girl from his father's collapsing frame. "I got it. Not sure how long, though."

"You need to just deal with it, son. I can't keep carrying her every time you break a sweat."

"This is bullshit. We should have just dumped 'er in the lake," Paul whined.

Devon froze and took a deep breath before approaching Paul. His eyes were serious—cold even. "We're not discussing this any further. Be a goddamn man for once," Devon said with anger in his voice. His fists clenched but never rose above his waist.

Paul remained silent. His face quivered with surprise and fear at the display of his father's aggravation.

"Now, shut the hell up and carry her," Devon added, turning back and glancing toward me.

Over the wind whistling and the scraping of tree branches around us, a new sound cracked through the air, stopping us in our tracks. A loud cracking. It rolled in from the darkness behind us, like a tree being twisted slowly at its trunk.

"What the hell was that?" Devon yelled out to me.

I remained still. The sound echoed through the landscape before fading back into the shadows around us. An idea was conjured from a dark place within me, begging to be validated. I refused to acknowledge it.

"Nothing. We need to move faster, though." I shifted my weight nervously, looking around but seeing nothing. Sweat beaded beneath my clothes. "Calm down, old man," I mumbled under my breath. "It's nothing."

Devon and Paul caught up, nervously watching their backs.

"That didn't sound like nothing, Grant," Devon said.

"I thought you said nothing lived here," Paul added.

"It was probably an old tree falling down. They get old, die, and rot," I explained.

"I'm not so sure about that, old buddy." Devon looked around, his eyes wide with unease.

From the sound of it, I wasn't exactly sure of it either. The place was old…ancient even. It was older than the trees blanketing its hellish landscape. My stomach had knotted with tension.

"We should get a move on," I said.

My eyes caught something snagged on a nearby tree limb. "What is that?" I said under my breath, stepping forward to get a closer look. It was a strip of old cloth, heavily soiled and frayed.

"Find something?" Devon asked, approaching to my side.

"Some kind of burlap, it looks like." I reached out to touch it as it waved in the breeze. The atmosphere had grown hazy in the low light. "Come on. We're losing light."

The trees thinned, and the ground grew rockier before I realized we were on the right path once more. The slow churning and bubbling sounds of water ahead guided my steps.

"We found it," I whispered.

"Found what?" Devon asked.

My feet picked up to a steady pace, once again leaving the other two trailing behind.

"Grant! Found what?" Devon repeated.

The faster I moved, the louder the canal got. The beast was waking, and suddenly, my memories came rushing back.

It was still here.

"Wait up. I can't move that quick," Paul said as his father left his side.

I stopped to wait for them. "It's up ahead just a li'l ways." I lit another smoke. The memories of the place had stirred up an apprehension that made my throat dry.

"What's up ahead? What are you talking about?" Devon asked.

The canal wasn't far from where I stood. My muscles ached and burned, yet I took odd comfort in knowing the other two were in worse shape.

"A canal. It runs to the mountain," I said.

"A canal? Like a river or something?" Paul said.

"Something like that...yeah. Not much farther to go."

Paul limped to a nearby tree after dropping the girl carelessly to the rocky ground. He bent at the waist and rubbed a cramp from his leg. "Grant, mind if I bum a smoke?"

My first instinct was to tell the kid to go fuck himself. I didn't, but I wanted to. Even a man on death row deserved a last and final smoke to send himself off.

Dead man walking, I thought before tossing him the half-spent pack.

"Why are we doing this? I mean, can't we just bury her anywhere out here?" Paul asked, lighting up.

I knew the question was coming, but it angered me no less. Paul was a weak man who always took the short-cuts. I took a long drag from my smoke and felt my body tense.

"Listen, you piece of shit. You want anyone to find this body?"

Paul's face dropped. "Uh, n—no. Of course not."

"Then you do as I say. Your old man came to me to make sure this body is never found," I told him with a scowl.

Devon quickly stepped to his son's side. "It's okay. We're okay. Just tired, is all."

My face was hot with anger. I couldn't stand the kid but backed off as Devon made an attempt to keep the peace between us. Soon enough, Paul would be gone.

We neared the edge of the wide canal cutting through the earth the entire length of what our eyes could see, disappearing into the distant, hazy terrain on either side of where we stood. Devon and Paul marveled at its construction, like I had the first few times I'd seen it. The design was so unnatural. Its wide and uniform appearance indicated an intention...a *purpose*...meant to trap whatever fell into it. It was evil. The water running through it appeared black, like midnight tar. The canal itself was lined with dark stones worn smooth as glass. Only God knew how deep this thing ran.

"The hell is this?" Devon asked, peering over the side. His head snapped back, and he quickly rubbed his eyes. "It stings and smells like shit."

The water had calmed and was running slowly, but it was only a matter of time before it woke back up.

"This is what we came here for." I paused, lighting a smoke. "Sort of." It terrified me to be standing so close to it.

Paul covered his mouth and nose with a single, cupped palm. "Man, what is that smell?"

"Sulfur," I said.

"Sulfur? Here? Isn't that what volcanoes smell like?"

"Not sure why. Nothing ever made sense here," I said.

"This looks like it was built in here. I mean, look how neatly designed it is. How it slopes down at the same angle and how it's smooth on both sides. I know architects and engineers who would struggle with this," Devon said, marveling at the strange waterway.

"Don't get too close. You fall in and you've had it. No getting you out of there." I refused to take a single step closer to the edge and instead backed away from the other two as they looked on in curiosity.

Devon and Paul turned back at me.

"So, what do we do now?" Devon asked.

"We need to follow this canal toward the mountain up ahead."

"That's it?" Paul asked. "Why can't we just toss'er in now?"

I looked him in his eyes—his weak, trembling eyes. They were full of concern that the heavy lifting wasn't over just yet.

"You'll see why," I said.

The mountain stood beside a large clearing, where we found ourselves under the blanket of a churning sky whose clouds had taken on a sickly green. There was no passage beyond the enormous landmark high above the water. It was a breathtaking sight indeed, suitable for a prize-winning oil painting, the way it sat there flanked by rocky cliffs and frigid water, encased in a thin veil of rolling mist. I would have appreciated the majesty of it all if I hadn't been aware of what was hidden inside.

I was tired; the cold and wet air had chilled me to the bone and exhausted me more than it was capable of doing before. Perhaps it was my age catching up with me.

The other two hung over the corpse like shivering, pale scarecrows caught in the cold frost of a winter's morning.

The canal fed into the blackness of a large cavern leading into the mountain. It was just as big as I remembered, enough to fit a tractor-trailer through with plenty of space on either side. I listened as slow currents of water echoed within the cavernous walls.

"This is unreal. Never seen anything quite like this before," Devon swept a hand through his hair.

"Yeah, it sure is something else," I said.

"So, where does it all go?" Paul bent at the waist to peek over the side without stepping closer.

The gust of air suddenly brushing by us filled my nostrils with a putrid stench of rancid water and dead earth.

"Something terrible," I uttered.

Devon turned away from the water and approached me. "What the hell are we doing here? I appreciate you helping us out in this situation, but I just don't get it," he whispered.

I took a moment to gather my thoughts. "That cave will take care of your problem."

I could tell by the look on his face, the answer was not satisfying.

"But how? I don't understand," Devon asked. He was close enough that the warmth of his breath licked the side of my face.

The sound of the lake captivated me. It was hardly audible from here, with a calm softness of distant waves pummeling the island's rocky shore. I didn't look at Devon. Instead, my eyes trained on Paul. "Anything that goes into that cave is gone...for good."

Devon looked at me, bemused. "Okay. So, what do we do?"

I knew he would eventually understand, just like I did so many years ago.

"Hey, is that a walkway or something going in?" Paul yelled, pointing to a narrow ridge running along the edge of the waterway.

"Sort of, but one wrong move and that's it." On second thought, I should encourage the bastard to go in. Poor footing on the wet stone and goodbye.

"Stay out of there, son," Devon yelled, warning Paul.

"We wait. That's what we do," I said.

The canal remained stagnant for nearly an hour. The two sat and spoke of things a crippled father and son relationship might bring about. I omitted myself from their company as I pondered my own thoughts.

Had I made the right choice to agree to this? The night Devon showed up at my doorstep had been spent like many others since Lori passed away. I had found myself once again staring into the dancing flames of that fireplace, questioning how the house felt so cold without her. The property we worked so hard to make ours had become a five-acre reminder of how life was truly unfair. Our home slowly became the mausoleum I now resided in.

Perhaps what bothered me more than Lori's absence was the knowledge I carried with me that death was only a step in a much bigger process. My understanding of death, as limited as it was, scared the hell out of me. Not for my own fate, but of Lori's. I could not be content knowing what I knew and seeing what I had seen. Where had she gone? Was she at peace? I pondered those thoughts daily, developing a near religious-like obsession that might have resembled lunacy to most. But for me, it was a pursuit of answers.

I recalled the late hour with its unusual stillness. Time had slowed, and the darkened corners of the house had somehow become strangely unfamiliar. Perhaps it had been fatigue, or just my mind getting away from me. I hadn't the energy or the desire to leave the chair or the fire. My eyes closed, and I inched closer to sleep as the instrumental magic of *Sleepwalk* played beautifully on the radio.

For that moment, I felt a little more at peace. *Just one more song, Lori. Give me one more song.*

My peace had been short lived, jolted awake in my chair by the sudden, unexpected knocking on the front door. It was Devon, dripping wet in the cold rain, with a desperate plea to help his son out of what I believed was no accident…

These thoughts came to an abrupt halt as the water slowly increased in intensity.

I waited briefly before standing as the canal came to life, rapids growing fierce and violent. The gaping maw sucked water in an unbelievable display.

"Grant, what the hell is going on?" Devon asked.

"This is what we were waiting for," I said, lighting a smoke. "Grab the body."

Without hesitating, the two moved into action, grabbing each end of the poor girl's corpse.

"Now, move to the edge of the canal and slide her in."

Devon paused, kneeling by her head, his lips moving in a quiet prayer.

"Come on. Can we just get this over with? I wanna get the hell outta here," Paul whined.

Devon looked up at his son with eyes full of remorse. "Of course, son…Of course."

The steady roar of the rapids had grown to deafening levels. The ground trembled beneath our feet. Terrified, I stood back as they brought the corpse, wrapped in its tarp, to the side as instructed. They eased it over, letting the grip of the water take her.

"Wow, look at it go. That water is strong as hell, eh?" Paul said with cringing excitement.

Within seconds, the corpse was ensnared by the powerful torrent and carried into the darkness.

"That's it. She's gone," I said.

"Jesus, Mary, and Joseph. What on earth is in there?" Devon backed away as the water reached a thunderous cacophony from deep within the bowels of the mountain.

"Something that shouldn't be," I replied, even though he likely couldn't hear me over the cave's monstrous sucking noise.

Paul watched in amazement as his troubles were flushed from his worries. Less amused was Devon. He seemed troubled by his son, taking in a deep breath and collecting his thoughts. It was at that moment I knew Devon had finally seen Paul for what he was.

He walked slowly to Paul's side and exchanged a few words.

It happened so quick—Devon reaching inside his jacket, his hand producing a revolver. My stomach tightened. A loud crack ripped into the air, and the muzzle flash licked the back of Paul's head. I jumped backward as the bullet punched through Paul's skull, sending him collapsing into the angry water below.

"Jesus Christ!" I yelled.

Devon lowered the pistol. Its chrome darkened with the clouds swirling in the sky above it.

"What the hell did you just do?" I asked.

He stumbled and collapsed to his knees, then sat in a path of dirt and dead grass. "He had to go, Grant." His eyes looked up to mine. "He...he was no good."

CHAPTER
- FIVE -

The grandfather clock tolled once more. The living room had grown darker, with only the fireplace and a dim table lamp providing light.

"Jesus, Grant. So, he killed his own son?" Trevor sipped from a near-empty glass.

"Yeah. Shot him right through the back of the head, like a fuckin' rabid dog," Grant explained before he broke out in a hysterical laugh. "Though...I would feel bad for the dog."

"Why the hell would he do it?"

"He was a weed. Long overdue to be pulled," Grant said. "Devon knew that. Probably knew it for a long time. I suppose he wanted to be the one to kill him before..." Grant stopped himself.

"Before what?" Trevor asked impatiently.

"I think he somehow knew I would do him in."

"Would you?"

"He was never making it off that island either way," Grant said, finishing his glass in a single drink.

CHAPTER
- SIX -

With the canal drifting back into a gradual slumber, silence had made its return, leaving me alone with a form of Devon I hadn't seen before. Something within him had broken.

"Devon," I choked out.

He ignored me and just sat there, deep in the thoughts of a man who had found himself in a dark enough place he was forced to kill his own son.

This place had gotten to him somehow…probably long before he even arrived.

"Devon, we need to get a move on," I said.

Lightning seared the sky behind us, followed by a thunderclap that made Devon jump and rise to his feet.

"I suppose we should get going," he replied, smacking dirt from his jeans. "This was the last thing he saw, Grant.

I wish it could have been different." He looked at the cave where his son's body had disappeared forever, never to see the light of day again. "What's in there? I need to know."

"I'll explain later. Right now, we need to go before it gets dark."

He grabbed Paul's bag and slung it over a shoulder. "All right...let's go."

We left behind the ghosts of his son and an unnamed girl. I tried not to think about what that meant, mostly for the girl's sake. She was an innocent victim in all this, like many of the others who had been buried here.

"Stay close. I don't need you getting lost out here," I said.

Devon was paying little attention to anything but the ground. Dark circles had formed under the man's eyes—he looked like shit. Exhaustion would be an understatement for the both of us at that point.

Beads of mist collected on my skin, mingling with beads of sweat running down my face.

"Getting dark," he said.

"Just pay attention to where you step. Don't wanna fall in there," I cautioned, pointing to the canal lying mere feet away.

"The smell is getting stronger. Like, really bad."

"Yep, sure is. First sign of the canal waking back up is that stench getting worse."

The water had started to slowly rise. Such a strange phenomenon it was. It rippled as if the ground beneath was vibrating. Within a few minutes, the water would be several feet higher, leaving maybe six feet or so to the top.

"What the hell is this? This isn't natural." Devon's voice was edged with panic.

"Long story. One that leaves more questions than answers."

A loud crack shot through the air. A far-off tree had snapped and crashed to the ground. My blood froze with the feeling we had been followed.

"Is that normal out here?" Devon asked.

"Nothing is normal here. Just keep going. We can't afford to sandbag now."

It was there, hidden within the shadows ahead. The bridge, fashioned with aging wood and stone. Narrow, with questionable integrity, it passed over the water below. We neared the decaying structure, and before I could make another step toward it, Devon stopped and grabbed my arm.

"Whoa, hold up, brother. You don't expect us to cross over that?"

"Listen, we won't make it back to the boat in time," I said.

His face hung with confusion. "In time? For what?"

"We can't be out here in the dark. We'll get lost for sure."

"Then where are we going exactly?"

"I know where we can hold up for the night," I said, lighting a smoke. "Nothing I would give five stars to…but it'll do."

"Out here? We're in the middle of fucking nowhere, man."

I looked him in the eyes. "Just trust me."

Beyond the bridge was where the true nightmare began. The ground was blanketed with a thick mist, the only way forward being an uneven path knotted with tree roots and shrubbery. Each step had become cautious, both of us carefully watching our footing.

"Christ almighty, what are those?" Devon asked.

Ahead of us, strange figures lined both sides of the widening pathway, barely obscured by a smoky haze.

"Don't worry. They are just scarecrows," I explained.

Scarecrows had been the best way to explain them, yet they were nothing like anything seen back on any farm. Each one had been strapped to a post constructed in a Y-shape, arms suspended outward. The bodies had been wrapped in a burlap-like material. Some of their faces had rotted away. But the smell...

Devon gagged when the stench overwhelmed him. "I'm gonna get sick. These aren't like any scarecrows I've ever seen."

The stench was sweet and rotten, like fermenting fruit but much worse. They had been spaced far apart, perhaps twelve feet. They numbered about a hundred or more.

I looked at Devon as he clutched his palm over his face. It wouldn't help. "They let us know we are going in the right direction," I said.

"Where to? Hell?"

"Something like that," I replied.

My jeans had soaked through completely, becoming cumbersome and heavy. Our movement had grown slow. I watched the light of the sun fade through the filters of an ever-darkening sky. The woods had ended, opening up to a large field.

"Foggy out here. Chilly too," Devon said, slowing his stride.

"Stay close. Don't venture off the path." My pack grew heavier by the minute. I was tired, and my legs were cramping.

We continued along the trail of scarecrows resembling tall specters hiding in the fog ahead.

"I don't like these things," Devon said with unease. His eyes locked on one of them as we passed. This one had a face made of a leather-like material. The eyes and mouth had been crudely carved. Its gaze seemed to follow us as we passed. "Creepy," he added.

The weight of Devon's grief had become apparent, but it was broken when he realized the ground beneath us had become an old cobblestone pathway.

Time had taken a toll on the crude passage, broken and uneven in spots where the earth had collapsed beneath. It snaked toward the ghostly remnants of man-made structures peeking from the thick walls of rolling fog.

"What the hell is that?" Devon asked, breaking his silence.

"An old fishing village."

He halted abruptly. "Grant, I thought you said this place was a secret."

Thunder clapped overhead.

"Don't worry. This place has been dead for a long time."

The fog nearest the outskirts of the town carried with it familiar peppery fumes, making my nose run.

"Jesus, my eyes. The hell is it with this place?" Devon asked, clearing his throat.

I coughed and gagged with the burning sensation, which was followed by a stagnant-water taste that made me want to puke. "It'll pass," I said, struggling to speak clearly.

Devon's reluctance was obvious. With the sun fading into dusk and a storm brewing at our heels, confusion had started to become agitation. "This is where we're supposed to stay?"

Through the fog, an unseen rusted gate swayed gently and clanged with the passing of a light breeze.

My ankle rolled as I stepped on an uneven stone covered in thick mud moss. "Shit!" I yelled out. "Yes, this is the only option we have."

"Watch your step," Devon said, in an attempt to either show concern or be an asshole—both very real possibilities at this point.

Irritation coursed through me as I tried to ignore the pain. "Watch my step? I can't see shit with this fog."

As if heaven sent, a sudden scuff of Devon's boot sent him tumbling to the ground. "God dammit!"

I reached out to him. "You okay?"

"Yeah...yeah, I'm fine."

"Should take your own advice."

Though his face was partially obscured in the fog, I saw him grin as I pulled him up.

"You always were an asshole, Grant."

I took little comfort in knowing this was my last visit. Each step beyond those iron gates brought me closer to something I both longed for and feared to see ever again. The village stood frozen in the time in which it was lost. It was a relic of sorts, with its stone and wood structures remaining after centuries of exposure.

The wide, stone path intersected in rows of small dwellings resembling rudimentary cottages built from dark, unfinished granite and warped timber. Dirt and decomposing foliage crunching underfoot, we made our passage to the village center, sending ghostly echoes down the otherwise silent corridor.

My memory failed to serve me as a giant formed within the slow rolling mist. With an aching pulse, I suddenly remembered the ominous feature.

How could I forget?

The massive stone monument erected in the village circle. A hooded figure with an outstretched arm holding a lantern in the direction of the nearby shoreline. Its material was so weathered in spots, it appeared as a ghostly apparition.

"What the hell is that?" Devon asked.

"Just a statue."

"Yeah, but of what?" He looked closer at it with morbid curiosity. "Strange."

I also marveled at the design, something I never understood. Was this even a statue of a person? Or was it the grotesque depiction of some cruel deity.

We stood there for a few silent moments, long enough to take in the strangeness of this *thing*.

Our silence was broken by the low rumble of distant but steadily approaching thunderheads.

"We should get moving," I warned.

Otherworldly fog slowly swirled around us in faint ribbons. The atmosphere had grown increasingly bleak as the light fell and the gates vanished from my sight. The first rows of small houses were nothing but broken shapes behind the mist. Standing among the dwellings, I momentarily questioned my own sanity for bringing us here. Each home was a bit different, but all were hauntingly decayed, adding a sinister touch to the already decrepit landscape surrounding us.

"What are we looking for?"

I took no interest in providing an immediate response to Devon's questioning and instead focused on finding proper direction inside the ghastly conditions. Beyond the monument stood more of the dirt-stained cottages. Another unseen window shutter creaked and cracked into a wall, while the wind passed down one of the narrow streets.

"That's it." I stopped and looked back to meet Devon's questioning eyes. "Right there." I gestured toward the tall dark shadow of the church. Part of me shifted deep inside. After all these years...

With legs weakened by growing anxiety, I stepped forward once more and guided us through the crumbling, narrow walkways. Ghostly whispers of the town's past carried through the air. My focus remained intact on the tall bell tower peeking over the rooftops. We would finally break free of the cramped proximity of the dwellings, finding ourselves standing on the outer edge of the decrepit churchyard.

"This is unreal." Devon patted my shoulder. "Just look at that architecture."

"Just a really old church, is all."

"What is that sound? Waves? Are we near water?" he asked.

I knew all too well what it was, and it gave me chills, knowing it lay just beyond. "A beach. It sits just past the church."

A bitter gust rolled in from the not-so-distant shoreline, biting at the bare parts of my face.

"Let's get inside."

Devon ignored me and wandered slowly in the direction of the beach, stopping about ten feet from where I stood. His hair danced carelessly in the breeze as he gazed upon the water.

"What's out there?" he asked.

"What do you mean?"

"The water. It looks...different. Look, right there." He pointed to a large patch of water darker than the rest.

"Drop-off. Deep one too. Probably hundreds of feet."

He walked closer, hesitating but curious. "No fucking way," he said with unease.

"What?"

"No...can't be." He walked quickly across the moss-covered stone, overgrown weeds, and crab grass blanketing the landscape.

"Devon, where the hell are you going? Get back here! We don't have time for this!" I yelled.

He only increased his fast walk to a light jog.

Devon moved quickly for an old man.

"What in the hell has gotten into you?" I said under my breath as I walked after him.

He disappeared behind a large rock along the shoreline. Seconds later, he reemerged, examining something.

"Devon. What the hell are you doing?"

"You see this?"

It didn't take me long. Next to where he stood was the tattered and stained blue tarp that had been wrapped tightly around the girl's dead body. The maelstrom had to be quite strong to rip that from her.

"Not possible," I said.

"How? I thought you said—"

"I know what I fuckin' said. That can't be the same one."

"It is, Grant. Where the hell is the body? Is that gonna wash up here too?"

"No chance." I looked back at the ghostly apparition of the imposing church tower soaring from the village. "We should get back up there."

"Is it safe?" Devon asked.

"Would you rather stay out here with that storm comin'?"

Devon looked briefly at the sky and nodded. "Okay, okay. Fair enough."

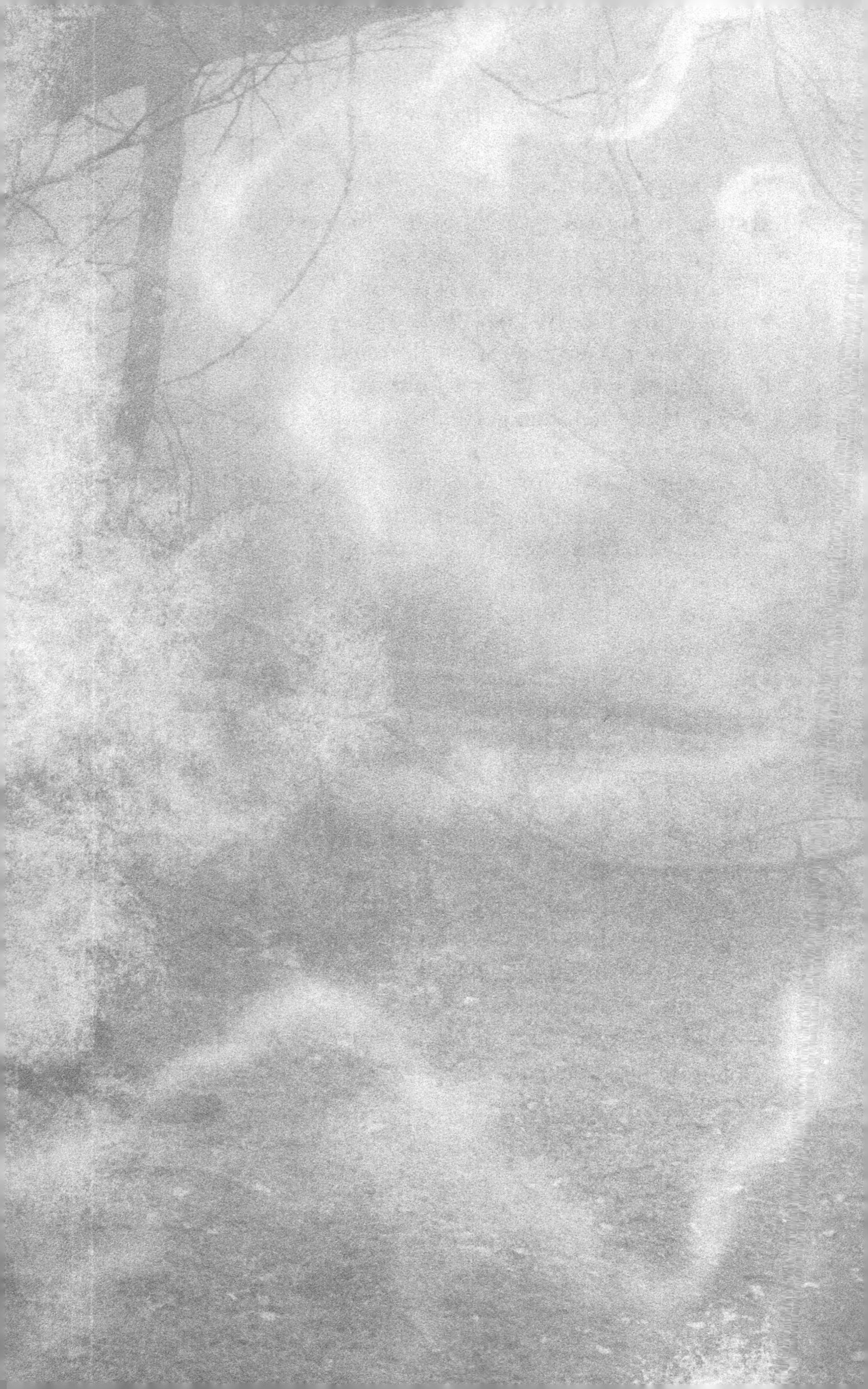

CHAPTER
- SEVEN -

The place was indeed dead. Knotted clumps of dried grass and weeds littered the ground. I could see the stone walk, stained green and brown in parts, as the icy fog curled and parted around me with every step.

The entrance had no doors, leaving instead just the large opening, with nothing to separate the outside world and the dark unknown inside. I had climbed the short flight of steps, and with a single deep breath followed by a slow exhale, I entered.

"Can't see shit in here," Devon said as his cautious steps traced behind me.

Ghostly rays of smoke-filled light pierced through the tall, grime-coated windows of the nave's unwelcoming interior. I recalled only minor details of the layout inside, trying hard to step carefully around broken, dry-rotted pews.

Devon followed, cautious and slow. Wood and dirt cracked beneath our feet and echoed throughout the dead stillness of the church. The air was musty and lingered with the odor of damp wood.

"Smells like an old basement."

I kept my silence as my eyes darted between the far spaces of the desolate room.

Devon continued, "I'm not a religious man, Grant. But this…"

It became clear to me rather quickly what had Devon spooked, what made him freeze behind me.

In the light's final moments before inevitable darkness stood a man-sized figure. This one was larger and much different than the ones outside. Crudely made, fashioned of cloth and rotted wood. Its face non-existent—a head of twigs, leaves, and dried grass shrouded in burlap. Masked in shadows, the scarecrow-like figure had been posed behind the deteriorating altar, as if to make a mockery of the church's former purpose.

Devon heaved in disgust, stepping closer and masking his face from the awful stench radiating from the twisted effigy. "In God's name…Grant, what the hell is this place? What happened here?"

My approach ceased in front of the twisted altar. I could almost feel it looking at me somehow, like it knew we were there.

"Where is it?" I fumbled through my pockets for the lighter. The flame bathed the darkness with orange as I searched around the grotesque figure. "Has to be somewhere…"

"What?" Devon asked, hesitant for his eyes to leave the tall thing standing watch over the altar. "You lookin' for something?"

The altar was decayed and warped to the point that its surface had sagged and bowed. But its cavity still appeared intact. I placed a single hand on the effigy. It felt damp and leathery.

"Look out."

With a strong push, the figure crashed to the floor, sending pieces of sticks and other materials across the dirty stone floor.

"What the hell are you doing, man?" Devon asked. His eyes questioned my every move as I fished into the bowels of the rotted altar.

"Has to be in here," I said. My hand gripped jagged pieces of wood that partially disintegrated under the slightest pressure. Beads of sweat ran into my eyes, stinging them. "I can feel it."

"Feel what? The hell are you talking about?"

My fingers swept across a hidden object. Smooth but textured, a surface dry like parchment. "Got it," I said, fighting to grip the binding from beneath a heap of rubble.

"What is that?" Devon asked in an accusing voice.

"Something I should have taken a long time ago," I explained, tucking the large book under my arm.

"I see. I take it they don't sell those at the bookstore back home?"

I walked past him. "Nope. One-uva' kind." The flame of my lighter danced in the dark window glass when I neared. "Come on. The rectory is back here."

Planks of wood groaned underfoot as we made passage up the small flight of stairs leading to the rectory. Through another door, we were finally greeted by the dark of a small room, with two windows facing the shoreline outside.

"This is it," I said.

"I can't see shit."

I smacked the iron body of a small wood stove occupying a far corner of the room. "Need something to burn."

As the storm approached outside, the church took on a life of its own, creaking and groaning. The onslaught of the blustery wind whistled, passing through hidden crevices. Although not the most favorable conditions for shelter, the structure itself was a testament to such dated craftsmanship. Inside the rectory, things were much more serene. Gore-Tex jackets hung over wood chairs.

I fought waves of exhaustion—this was no time to give into fatigue. Devon stirred the small fire and tossed in another piece of the church's ancient furniture, sending a shower of sparks cascading through the dark. The room was smoky and made my eyes tear with a mild sting.

Outside, the shoreline grew angry with the storm looming overhead. Amidst the flashing sky, I watched the surf in morbid amusement. The cherry of my cigarette glowed in the window as another gust of wind gripped the shoreline, sending monstrous waves crashing against the rocks. Thunder cracked outside.

"Good luck in this mess," I said, leaving the window and resting in a creaky old wood chair.

"Grant. Now that we're here, mind shedding some light on something?"

Here it was. The line of questioning. "What do you want to know?"

"That canal. This place..."

"Yeah, I guess I owe a bit of explanation." An ocean of thoughts ran through my head. None of them could easily explain what he wanted to know.

"What the hell was in that cave?"

My head nodded against my will, and the tightness in my chest returned. Time for another smoke. A quick spark of the lighter and a nice long drag got my gears working for what I was about to tell. "This place has been discovered time and time again over the centuries. The last being sometime during prohibition."

"By who?" he asked.

"My grandfather. He was a murderer and a bootlegger. This island has a way with making sure the right people find it," I explained.

"What?"

"Everyone who finds this place…they aren't exactly the kind of men who take their kids to soccer games and volunteer for carpools. Somehow, it knows who needs it and draws them in."

"I see…and that makes you…"

"A garbage man. For men like you."

He grinned. "All those years, I never asked how you did it. Ya know, men like me need guys like you," he explained.

"You mean murderers."

Devon looked to the floor and nodded. "Yeah. You make lots of enemies in my line of work. You know that."

"You always paid well. That's all that mattered to me."

He looked at me once more. "So, when did you take over the family business?"

"My dad started taking me out here after 'Nam. Told me it was easy money. Probably the same shit his dad told him. It wasn't easy. Sometimes, we would even lose people."

Devon's face took on an expression of confusion. "Lose? How?"

"It was my third time out with the crew. My dad was a very secretive man, and he would have me stay on the boat, to keep watch while he and the others ventured out with the cargo. Normally, they would come back without the cargo. But one time, they came back one man short."

The ground beneath my chair vibrated in concert with the sudden outburst of thunder claps. Without hesitation, I stood and walked to the window, surveying the beach once more underneath an angry sky.

"What happened?" Devon asked.

"His name was Ernie Ragland. Dad came back that day mad as hell. Said Ernie was an idiot for standing so close to the edge of the canal."

"Did he fall in or something?"

I returned to the chair, my aching back resting against its wood frame. "The current was too strong. Sucked him right in."

"What's in there, Grant?"

I pictured it before answering. "The abyss. Something you'd never wish to see."

Devon leaned toward me. "But you saw it, didn't you?"

My deep breath could have been mistaken for nervousness. And maybe I was. Either way, dredging up the images proved tasking. "With a man short, my old man had no choice but to take me off the boat on the next trip out. Told me that it was just animal carcasses, like deer hit in the road, and the state paid him for disposal. I knew he was full of shit, but I kept quiet about it. He took me on the same route I led you on. I remember waiting a bit after we got there. The water was calm, just like you saw, and then it started to pick up. One of the guys asked me if I wanted to see inside."

Devon grinned. "Buddy, I appreciate the suspense, but come on."

"They called him Ox. Big ol' son of bitch from Kentucky. The type of guy who got off on thrills and was looking for a reason to go check it out again. I remember how his voice was so loud in there, and how, even with our flashlights, we had a difficult time seeing where we were going on that little ledge. We walked slowly, and after about ten minutes, we finally reached a point where the cave sort of opens up into this large chamber. That's where the canal ends in a huge pool." I lit another smoke and surveyed the remaining contents of the pack before tucking it back into my pocket. "Ox told me to crouch beside him, and then we waited. Things were pretty uneventful for a bit, until I started to feel a strange vibrating sensation from the ground. Thought it was just my imagination at first. Then it got stronger. Felt like the whole damn thing was gonna collapse on us. He must have seen the look on my face because his big, meaty hand gripped my shoulder fiercely, and he yelled in my ear to watch the water. It churned and frothed violently, roaring with such fury. Waves tossed up over the rocks where we kneeled, water sprayed my face, and all I could do was brace the deck and dare not move a muscle."

"Like an earthquake or something?" Devon asked.

"No. Not an earthquake. Nothing like that. The roaring started to subside and was replaced by another sound. It paralyzed me with terror. Distinguishable slurping coming from somewhere in the dark. I didn't realize I had my eyes closed until Ox slapped my leg and yelled for me to look where his light was. The water appeared to have fallen in on itself, forming a wide funnel. My mind was not ready to fathom such a sight."

"A whirlpool?" Devon asked.

"The largest I had ever seen. The whirl was big enough that it could swallow a large boat with ease. Anything that gets caught in that thing would be gone forever. I shudder knowing that was Ernie's final moments."

Devon's face signaled his intrigue. "How does something like that exist here? I mean, even that canal looks like it was put there for a purpose."

"Not sure. This village was built by the unlucky souls who tried to settle here. Some of the older natives have their legends about it, and the ones who know won't go near the place."

"What happened here?"

I shrugged. "All I heard was, they began throwing their own into that canal."

"Jesus. Why?" Devon asked.

I lit a smoke as bright flashes pierced the window glass. Cracks of thunder followed within seconds. "Rituals, I suppose. Sacrifices."

"Weren't they Catholics? I mean...this church and all."

"I imagine they were when they settled here. Until the place changed them."

"They worshipped the whirlpool?" he asked.

"Not exactly. More like whatever is on the other side."

Devon sat up, looking pensive, his eyes unfocused as he digested what he had heard. "The other side?" he asked.

"A god of sorts. They believed that the whirl was a passage or gateway to the afterlife."

The rectory briefly filled with the strobe of lightning flashes. The wind howled through the cracks and crevices in the walls with brief but intense gusts.

"So, they just tossed folks in and hoped for the best?"

"That's my understanding. Dead and alive."

"Dead?" His eyes widened. They had a baffled and oddly curious look in them.

"Did you happen to see a graveyard out there?"

Devon looked back at me with a bewildered expression on his face. "I guess I didn't," he said, looking uncomfortable and fidgeting with his hands. "So Paul..."

I stopped him before he could finish. "It's just legend and myths, my friend. Try not to think about it."

He eyed the pack of smokes sitting on the floor beside me. "Mind if I get one of those from you?"

Devon stood into a stretch. "Wish I'd brought cards or something to pass some time, at least. Speaking of which. What time is it? My watch stopped."

A growling stomach and anxious boredom prompted me to retrieve my last cereal bar from my bag. The small room had grown more familiar over the hour, and small talk all but ceased. Our fire had already eaten a good amount of the broken wood and timber found around the church's blackened interior. Outside, the storm had reduced itself to heavy rain and occasional thunder, providing a more peaceful element to an already bleak atmosphere.

I looked at my watch and tapped on its face, knowing it hadn't worked in years. "Not sure."

The rain fell rhythmically against the old roof, creating a tranquil mood inside the small rectory.

The crack of the fire caught Devon's attention. "Guess we should go find more wood," he said, before heading to the narrow rectory door. "I'll see what I can find."

I sat idly in that wood chair, looking into the fire. A calm blaze, like the fire I sat by on the night of her funeral. Lori had loved the fireplace. She'd looked forward to winter as an excuse to use it. Those bitter nights where the air froze and the snow fell, we'd always stayed in and kept the fire going. She would sit there in its glow, reading away. Nights like that reminded me how content I was. At peace.

I wondered exactly why I was here. My intent was lost and no longer in focus. With Paul dead, all that remained was Devon. Vengeance aside, this was the only way I could possibly see…

The door snapped back open, revealing Devon once more with an arm full of splintered wood. He fed some into the stove and sat down.

"Hey. I really do appreciate everything you've done for—"

"Devon, stop. You don't need to—"

"No, Grant, I do. I know you've been through a lot these last few years. Hell, we haven't really talked much since… since Lori passed."

"Now isn't the ideal time to be catching up," I said.

"You know I cared about Lori too. I attended her service. I didn't know what to say to you after that. You kind of…"

"Faded out. I sure did."

"But why? I didn't see you talk to anyone that day."

"I wish I had caught on sooner, not taken time with her for granted. Of course, Lori's beauty was matched only by her stubbornness, especially when it came to her health. I should have known something was wrong when she started asking me to go with her to the grocery store. I now carry so much regret that I missed all that I did. Then one weekend, she came to me in the cool of the morning as I had my coffee on the porch. She sat beside me and placed her hand on mine and asked me with that pleading voice one more time. So, I went."

"To the store?"

"We walked the aisles. I pushed the cart for her, and she explained it all to me. Where things were, what brands she bought, and the days of the week to get the best deals. I caught on that this trip wasn't just for her pleasure. She was teaching me the things I needed to know to take care of myself the way she had for the better part of forty years. I never felt a broken heart before that day. I missed so much in the early days of the sickness. The signs. She knew it before the doctors did."

"Jesus, Grant."

"She'd told me on a Friday, which was always our day. I couldn't remember the last time we'd missed a date night. I'd asked her that afternoon as she sat in the kitchen. She would usually be dressed up and ready to go, but not this time. Instead, she sat at the table with a folder in front of her. I hated that folder. It held the news I never wanted. I can't remember exactly how I reacted, but when I think of that folder...I just can't."

"I—I'm sorry, man. I can't imagine how you feel. I haven't spoken to Paul's mother in years. I could care less if I did. I suppose what I'm trying to say is that you were blessed to have someone like Lori. The memories you have will always be there."

I looked at my wedding band, grinned, and chuckled. "Yeah. I suppose you're right. At least until my old ass gets dementia."

Devon laughed. "You and me both, old man."

Suddenly, my focus came in sharper than before. With the cracking of the fire filling the silence that followed, I could only remember why I was really here. I lit a smoke and began to process these thoughts, watching Devon rub his tired eyes, accompanied by a muted yawn.

"You know...I was gone the day she died. I should have been there," I said.

The corners of his mouth narrowed as his smile faded. He had shifted into sudden discomfort with my bringing it up.

"I'm sorry. How was I supposed to know?"

My face dropped, and my eyes met the dirty floor in front of me. "She was forced to spend her last days with a nurse who hardly knew her."

His sigh was loud and forceful. "I was waiting for this to come up someday. I never knew what I would say when it did."

"It was your goddamn son...wasn't it? Tell me it was Paul."

Devon sat up, surprise washed over his face. "How'd you know?"

I looked into his eyes and saw a reflection of the stove's dancing flame. "That girl, just like the one we brought here today, had been strangled."

"After all these years"—he swallowed nervously—"you dare accuse my son..."

"He was a fucking murderer, and you know it!"

"You don't know that," he said.

"I saw the marks on her neck. Why else would you have shot him?"

Devon swallowed hard and nervously rubbed the back of his head. "You...you looked?"

"After you brought her onto the boat...yes. This was no accident, just like the ones before. Just like the one who caused Lori to be left alone with a stranger in her final days. I should have been there."

Shame filled the man in front of me. The room had gone cold and uneasy.

The moment I had been waiting for was near.

CHAPTER
- EIGHT -

We sat in uncomfortable silence, each one waiting for the other to break it. The fire cracked, and the world outside remained dead and quiet, with the exception of an occasional slam of a shutter or loose door crashing against its twisted frame. My patience was being tested, along with my nerves. After all, this was the first time I'd willingly stuck around for it.

With the dying of the fire and the creep of the hour, I waited. My thoughts carried me through the passing moments that followed. It was almost as if the weather had died down entirely to set the stage…

I jumped from the chair when the bell tolled loudly overhead.

Ding!

The haunting sound quaked around us.

Devon sat frozen in his seat, wide-eyed and visibly alarmed. "What the—"

Ding!

The death knell rang out again.

"Grant, what the hell is going on?"

My throat went dry with the knowledge of what was coming. One more…

The silence hung in the air felt like an eternity before…

Ding!

The final toll echoed through the dark chambers of the church, expanding over the decayed village and across the waters into the cold, endless reaches of night.

I took post beside the window once more.

"Grant. I asked you a question. What the hell was that?"

"The bell. Nothing more." My hands shook as I lit a cigarette. "Nothing to worry about."

Devon's posture became more confrontational. "You look spooked. Why do I get the feeling you're not telling me something?"

The sky had cleared way for the bright white of the full moon. A thick, icy fog hugged the ground.

"It's nothing," I said.

I grew skeptical of my own intentions, until the moment I anticipated this whole time had arrived. Summoned by the death knell, broken shapes formed in the darkness behind the shroud of lingering fog. Slowly and deliberately, I watched as more of them rose from the cold, black water.

"The abyss holds them…until the bell calls," I said.

I felt Devon's eyes on my back. "What are you talking about?"

"The bell—it calls out to the dead."

"The hell are you saying?" Devon approached me from behind and grabbed my shoulder. "You need to start making some damn se—"

His words were cut short as he looked outside.

It was like a coming storm, slow but deliberate.

"Wha—who? What's going on?" Devon backed away from the window. "You knew about this. What did you do? Where the hell are we?"

"They called it Purgatory for a reason."

The slow-moving crowd of barely visible figures were closing in from the beach. They must have numbered close to a hundred, each of them a cloaked, soggy corpse moving within the creeping mist. Their burdened forms lumbered beneath tattered clothing blackened from decay and filth.

The church had come under siege. They filled the nave with horrible sounds that could only come from torn and rotted throats. The small rectory became a room less personal than before. It no longer served as a shelter. Within mere moments, we had simply been reduced to invaders of this dead and cold space.

Devon paced around the rectory nervously. "I'm leaving this damn place. You can rot here for all I care, but I'm getting to that boat."

I remained silent, watching Devon reduce himself to a scared man about to make a grave decision. He was nothing more than a shadow in that dark room as he searched and shuffled, sending unseen things into the wall nearest the window.

With a sudden loud snap, the old window busted. Another followed with a much louder crash. A bigger object had been hurled through it, and the window was shattered.

The night air rushed in, along with much clearer moans of the dead. They didn't seem to react to the window breaking—no heightened excitement, just the parade of death still making its way from the cold reaches of the tide.

Devon neared the opening, propping himself up and preparing to jump out. "You better hope I don't see you again, old friend," he said, before disappearing into the darkness outside.

I sat in that dirty corner and waited, alone once more… cold *and alone*. The sounds outside the rectory door drew nearer. The corpses were slow, dragging themselves along with a frightening degree of persistence. I watched the door, waiting. Any moment, it would swing open and in would enter ghouls, decayed and blackened with tattered rags hanging from dead limbs.

But the door never crashed open.

Not even a knock would befall the only barrier between me and those…things. In fact, the commotion had all but ceased, leaving only faint sounds of shambling and throaty growls.

CHAPTER
- N I N E -

As time passed in its eternal crawl, I shivered with the blanket of cold, bitter air encircling me. The rotten stench of the dead carried within it. They had to know I was here, waiting for them. Why did they make me wait?

The dark hid me, but the dead were not limited by mortal senses. They would know I had been here. Lori would know.

I was shaken by the sudden chaos of yelling outside. It was distant but coming closer.

Devon.

His words could not be made out, but he was both terrified and scared. I stood and walked to the broken window. He likely didn't make it far.

They carried him back to the church, and his frightened, incoherent screams filled the nave. My curiosity drew me close to the door. I took little care in being silent as I lifted away the boards and furniture Devon had hastily thrown in place.

The door creaked, rubbing against the warped frame. A powerful stench struck me. It was putrid and turned my stomach. From my vantage point, I saw them—a large collection of soggy corpses now occupying the church, their silhouettes barely visible in the blue hue of moonlight cutting through the rows of stained glass. But it was Devon who shocked me most; he had been lashed to a post, like the ones we saw on the way in with the scarecrow figures on them. His arms stretched overhead.

They just watched him. Their noises echoed through the walls of the church and mingled with the moans of the hundreds still wandering outside. He was exhausted and had little fight left in him. I couldn't help but stand in morbid curiosity, and I would be lying if I said I wasn't a bit terrified at this display. I had never seen this before.

I wondered if Lori was there. Would she be just as rotten and twisted as the others? Maybe she was different. I hoped she was different.

We were all there in that dismal place...me, Devon, *them*...and a noise caught my attention. It didn't come from inside the church, but outside, in the distant woods. Branches and tree trunks cracking and crunching, being ripped apart. My skin crawled and trembled with the realization that whatever was doing this had been making its way to the village. I couldn't control my terror. Whatever it was, it had to be big. Much bigger than the corpses littering the area.

It came from deep within the woods—something I hadn't seen before. Its approach had been signaled not only by the snapping of thick tree limbs, but also the dead standing in unison. My breathing remained heavy, and my limbs quaked with a thundering pulse.

Devon had gone silent, likely in shock. From where I stood, I could barely make him out in the darkness, instead seeing more of the twisted post holding him. The place smelled rotten with death, and the air had grown humid from the crowd of festering wet flesh.

The church had gone quiet; not a breath nor a single mournful wail dared to break it. The setting felt like some terrible dark mockery of a Sunday service, and I no longer wished to be here. Lori could be mere feet from where I stood, and I had a sudden onset of newfound pity for what I had doomed her to be forever.

I could leave…maybe go out the window like Devon.

Before I could take a single step back, the large doors to the church slammed open, and I jumped. I couldn't take my eyes off it—a tall and slender shape entering the church with slow, menacing steps. Details were few inside the lingering darkness, aside from the cascade of long hair draping its head.

It had passed between the pews, approaching Devon with a cruel purpose. I watched the dark space it occupied in front of the post, listening to its sick, inhuman whispers.

Devon groaned as if bothered by an ache…He then coughed and spat as the hulking figure stepped away. As if part of a strange ritual, some of the dead had joined Devon's side, a small group of them surrounding him.

They gripped the post and lifted it, disappearing back into the darkness.

"Where the hell are you taking me?" Devon asked.

His legs kicked helplessly against the heavy post he had been lashed to. The corpses followed behind the tall figure, making the exit from the church.

The sound of movement was all around me—sloshing steps of an approaching...*thing.* The moonlight caught some of them, and I jolted back against the frigid surface of a stone wall. The water had pruned their flesh to the point it looked like wrinkled tar clinging to bone. Their eyes had rotted away into darkened pits. Whatever clothes they bore in their last moments of life were now tattered strips, replaced by slime, filth, and sea grass. Many of them remained partially covered in crude burial shrouds—the village's original occupants.

There in the darkness, something came close. I couldn't see it, but it had crept closer to me with that terrible sloshing noise. A raspy sound came from rotted vocal chords... Wet gurgling followed. The light finally caught it, and I couldn't believe what I saw. The hair stood up on my arms, and I lost the ability to breathe without screaming. Quickly, I jumped back and ran blindly toward the rectory, until I smacked my face against the wooden door.

The pain didn't come...not then at least. I felt nothing as I swung the old door open and shut it behind me. My sight had blurred, and I stumbled to a chair before collapsing into it like a helpless marionette. Darkness swallowed my vision...

I couldn't see when I came to. Nothing but darkness filled my vision. But I could feel something, the odd sensation of being manipulated, squeezed, and carried.

"No. You—" I tried to speak.

They had a hold of me. Their hands felt like sponges wrapped around bone, and my arms couldn't move. I could feel them hanging to my side, my fingers brushing across the tops of weeds.

A foul smell crept into my nostrils, a wretched odor of rot and putrid water. My head began to swim once more. "No—"

My eyes would open again, but this time, I knew I had been carried into the woods. All around me, their hellish moans filled the cold night air. The march was slow—they were dead and moved accordingly. Somewhere along the way, whether it had been ten minutes or half an hour, I didn't know, but I regained my senses and encountered renewed terror upon realizing what their intentions were.

"No," I said, struggling to get air into my lungs.

A peppery tinge wafted through the air, mingling with the rancid stench of the dead, sending me into a coughing fit. Then I heard him...Devon. He was up ahead, coughing and shouting at the dead that carried him. I tried to look around but couldn't see him, only shadows and mist.

"Let me go," I said, trying to shake from their grip.

They didn't even look at me as I yelled. They were emotionless. Pity was not something they could experience here.

"Please, let me go," I begged, looking at one of them directly, hoping it would somehow listen.

Its face was covered in burlap that was torn in places. I tried not to look too deep within its shroud.

"Get me off of this thing now!" Devon yelled. He was far ahead of me, judging by the faintness of his voice.

The procession moved at an agonizing pace. All I could do was listen to Devon's screams as we were paraded through dense woods, and then I heard it...

The waters of the canal filled the night with a thunderous quake. The beast had awakened once more. The smell of sulfur lingered.

"Get your hands off of me!" I yelled again, struggling to break free of their hold without any luck.

The canal was stirring, churning, and tossing its rapids to my right. My suspicions had proven true…

They were taking us to the mountain.

The sky opened above when we cleared the trees. My vision filled with the hazy moonlight cascading through peeks from large clouds. The rapids had only grown louder and angrier as I was carried near the mountainside.

"What the fuck are you doing?" Devon yelled, and the shambling corpses halted.

Within an instant, I was dropped to the ground. The dead moved around me, all facing one direction. With my elbows, I crawled backward slowly to avoid their attention, navigating through the gauntlet of legs until reaching a clearing. My chest ached with the pain of adrenaline and terror, but I managed to get to my feet. In front of me was an army of ghouls—all of them looking to the mountain in a strange observance of what was to happen next.

I watched as Devon's post was picked up, his limbs still restrained, and moved to the edge of the canal. The tall figure, draped in some kind of shroud, stood nearby.

"You son of a bitch, Grant. I know you're out there," Devon yelled.

The tall figure took him, wrapping its long arms around the post in a snake-like hug. Devon tried to yell, but the air had been squeezed from his chest. The mysterious figure walked him to the canal's edge, paused, and then took a single step forward, sending both itself and Devon into the treacherous waters below.

It wouldn't take long for them both to be swept into the maelstrom waiting inside. Then suddenly, many of the corpses followed them in. Dozens of them walked off of the edge and into the canal. Some others turned around, facing me, and my heart jumped with horror as they moved slowly to close the distance between us.

Without hesitation, I turned and ran in the only direction I could. The canopy quickly choked out what little light the moon provided.

"Sons o' bitches, you're not gonna…" I ran blindly through thick brush. My chest burned mercilessly, and I struggled to catch a breath, which eventually forced me to stop.

I took the opportunity to listen, fighting to hear beyond my heavy breathing.

Nothing.

"Where are you? Did they give up?" I asked in a whisper.

Silent moments passed before a sudden snap whirled through the air.

Then another, and another.

They were coming.

With my pursuers closing in, I forced myself to run. I moved as quickly as I could, catching jabs and cuts of hidden sticks and branches along the way.

"Shit!" I yelled, plummeting the slope of a ravine. I crashed into twisted branches and wet leaves, narrowly dodging a large tree. Attempting to stand sent a jolt of pain through my leg. "Son of a—" I shouted, falling onto a knee.

In the dark, I blindly examined my leg to make sure everything was intact. All felt fine, but my knee was throbbing terribly. I fought through it, standing once more, and hobbled up the steep slope of the ravine, using whatever tree possible to ease my climb upwards.

The dead continued their slow but dogged pursuit, gaining ground, their discordant moans reminding me to not slow my pace.

Exhaustion had reached a new level I had never experienced before. I froze when I heard it—the sound of waves crashing against rocks. I was both relieved and nervous. I had made it, but what if the boat wasn't there, I thought.

"It'll be there. Not much farther to go," I said to myself, pushing forward, following the sounds of the surf.

I moved with a subtle limp. I ached, pain shooting through me with each step. And then a sharp pain engulfed me like fire. I had been caught in the webbing of the nightmarish thorn bushes lining the forest perimeter. Without thought, I pushed and pulled my way through them.

"Goddamn things!" I yelled, breaking free of the barrier and crashing to the black sand of the beach. It smelled terrible, but I didn't care—I made it.

I couldn't see much in the darkness of the early morning and had been unable to detect the trawler. Without light, I couldn't get a bearing on where I was.

Should I go left or right? Where the hell am I?

It wouldn't be long before the dead caught up. The woods behind me cracked and moaned.

"Come on, come on," I said, scrambling up and down a small section of the island's coastline. All I could see were nearby rocks…This was the wrong spot. "Maybe farther up."

The sand beneath my feet gave way under my weight as I ran. I had only the sickly glow of moonlight shimmering along the distant water to guide me. The snaps of branches and brush grew louder…They were closing in on me.

I dared not look toward the trees as I carefully ran along the coast line, the tide lapping at my legs. The dead were out there. Their wet moans had gotten more intense upon clearing their way through the thorn bushes. Without hesitation, I ran at an angle and found myself knee-deep in freezing water, robbing me of my breath.

"Where the hell…Come on," I said, looking around for a sign the trawler was there.

In the distance, a dim pair of red lights bobbed against a backdrop of darkness.

"There you are."

As if running in mud, I stepped wildly into waist-high water and pushed myself deeper, until I could no longer touch the bottom. I had found myself over another drop-off. The unimaginable depths sent chills through me as I fought to clear the slope and gain a footing beneath the water.

"Come on, old man. Push it," I said to myself, swimming with the help of a current that drew me closer to the glowing beacon.

Once I reached the trawler, I blindly felt around for the ladder to climb aboard and pull in the anchor, which took all the remaining energy I had.

They got close to me this time. The closest they had ever come.

As I sat in an ocean of terror, I could feel them out there on the shoreline, their dead eyes looking at me from the darkness.

It gave me chills knowing Lori was among the vast gathering of walking corpses.

CHAPTER
- TEN -

Trevor's face wore the look of disbelief. He couldn't simply believe what he had heard and, for obvious reasons, had been tempted to call Grant out on such ridiculousness. The hour had grown late, and the fire cracked and spat embers.

"Grant…I'm having trouble—"

"Believing it," Grant said, cutting him off.

"Uh, yes. I mean," he fumbled in his words. "An island where dead people walk around. I'm sorry, but this sounds too—"

"Yeah, I know." Grant lit a freshly cut cigar. "Faith. Have faith. This place I told you about, it's as real as any other."

Trevor choked down a shot of whiskey and grimaced. "Jesus, strong stuff." He placed the glass down and thought before speaking. "Why am I here? If this is all true, what left is there?"

Grant nodded, puffing at his cigar. "I'll show you," he said, standing up and walking to the next room.

Trevor sat in silence, listening to the cracking of the fire and the ticking of the nearby clock hidden from view. Minutes would pass before Grant reemerged from the dark of the neighboring room with an old, tattered briefcase, its leather faded and rubbed in spots.

"I put it in here," he said as he sat. "The book I told you about...from the church." With a faint click, the brief case came apart ever so slightly. Grant lifted the top and produced a book that appeared older than anything Trevor had ever seen.

"What the hell?" Trevor couldn't believe what he was seeing. The binding was a blackened leather material. It emitted an odor of something terrible.

"Inside here is something people have searched over centuries to find," Grant explained. His hand hugged the spine, and he opened the relic. The binding made a cracking sound as the jagged and darkened pages were exposed.

"That's pretty great and all. Give it to a museum, make a few bucks, and get on with life," Trevor said.

Grant looked up, his eyes meeting Trevor's. "No," he said, closing the book gently. "I need a favor."

Trevor's face hung in surprise. "A favor? Like what?"

"I need you to deliver something. When the time comes, that is," Grant said, puffing away at his cigar. Smoke rolled by his aged face in shimmery curtains.

"What?" Trevor asked.

"This won't be easy for you, but if you can do it, I'll give you all of this," Grant said, holding his arms up. "House and everything."

"Grant, what the fuck are you talking about?"

"My days are coming to an end." Grant pressed the cigar into the ashtray and let it smolder. "I'm no good lying 'round here all day and night anyways."

"Jesus, Grant. You make it sound like you're dying or something."

"Cancer," Grant said, lifting a shot glass in the air. "The only thing that could catch Grant Radburn."

Trevor's hands massaged his face and scalp. "Man. I'm sorry to hear that, but can't you —"

"No. No treatments. No chemo. No doctors. You'll know when the time comes." Grant put the book back in the brief-case. "I'll have directions for you. Carry me up to that canal and dump me in."

"Carry you? Dump you in? I can't believe what I'm hearing," Trevor said.

Once again, the grandfather clock chimed. It was louder than before. Midnight had fallen upon them.

"You're the only one I have left that could. Dump me in and get out of there," Grant said.

Trevor knew deep down he had been drawn into something inescapable. With a strong sip of bourbon from the unlabeled decanter nearest Grant, he nodded in agreement.

CHAPTER
- ELEVEN -

Six months had passed since that night. I was with him when he passed on a warm summer evening. He was watching the lightning bugs against the backdrop of a darkened pink sky, and then before the fiery sky went black, he fell silent.

The next morning, I took off. It was a long trip through the north, heading for the remote pier where I met a stranger, one who gave me a small fishing boat dated beyond its years.

With the maps, I found the place Grant spoke of. I never would have known it to exist had I not been given such vital information. The place was truly terrible, and I nearly abandoned the entire request altogether. But I went through with it. I carried his ass through the woods and respected his last wishes. It was late afternoon when I slid him into those angry waters. I couldn't imagine Devon going in that alive.

I returned to the boat and made a circle around. After the sun fell, I waited in the shroud of fog until that certain hour stroked and the death knell tolled over the ghostly village of Purgatory. I then approached and set anchor.

Accompanied only by a case of beer and a pack of smokes, I sat and listened. Their moans carried along the wind if the gust blew in just right. I could feel them out there, watching me with those dead eyes—rotting, black pits all pointed in my direction, hoping they could feed me to the maelstrom.

May God keep this place hidden from the world.

www.ingramcontent.com/pod-product-compliance
Lightning Source LLC
Chambersburg PA
CBHW070508170726
48291CB00008B/2697